I0658118

the broken toys we keep

episodes

by m. a. white

Copyright © 2024 by m. a. white. All rights reserved.

This book or any portion thereof may not be reproduced or used in any manner whatsoever without the express written permission of the author.

Printed in the United States of America

First Printing, 2024

ISBN 978-1-955791-97-7

pref•ace:
it always began with a door opening
and ended with bodies fizzling into stardust
everything else was an accident

episode 1

nothing

has

looked

right

ever

since

the front door of the opera house bookstore had a sign on it
which read:

it's a pull!

i always thought that was unnecessarily kind and ultimately
human.
no doubt, enough employees had watched enough customers
push their faces flat against an unmoving door, to feel that
something needed to be done.

so, someone or a group of someones, thought to grab an
index card and write in bold sharpie the orientation of the
hinges on their front door.
they're still in business.

it took me about half an hour to walk there every morning
from my apartment. i'd recently dropped out of college and
was getting over a bad breakup.
before that, i was working at american airlines and also spent
some time at walmart and starbucks, too.
i knew nothing. so, i read a lot.
and they had countless novels written by sad men trying to
save the world. unfortunately, i was very broke and couldn't
afford the many reasonably priced secondhand books.

so, i would steal them.

it was a two-story building with fiction on the second
floor. i would look around as unnoticeable as i could. grab
the title i wanted. and stuff it in my pants really quick.
walking out.
pushing the door and me into the sunny world.

i'm happy to say that i no longer shoplift.
not for any moral reason but because i'm just more afraid
of getting caught.
proof that we don't need religion to follow the rules. just
more jails, evidently.

i would usually take my stolen book to the coffee shop
near my place and pretend to read and drink coffee.
the pretending to read was so i could watch people. or i'd
look at the shit carved in the tables.
occasionally, i would actually read.

it depended on the crowd what i paid attention to.

from there, i would walk across campus and give plasma
to scare up a little drinking money for the night.
they paid decently and i got all my blood back. the only
thing i didn't like was by the time the blood got back in
my body it was chilly cold like ice filling me up.
but i got used to it.

about that time, classes let out and the bars would swell
with people.

the chatter got louder.

laughter bounced off tables.

and i'd sit and drink beer... it was like a still life painting of familiar things that were slightly off. like shadows hitting the wrong walls for where the light should be. it was all funhouse mirrors back then.

and nothing has looked right ever since.

inevitably, someone would come up.

in this case, it was calliope.

she was a theater major who had an older guy with her named timothy. grown up dude named timothy that dressed like the crocodile hunter and would hang on calliope like a scaly purse.

timothy was creepy.

-hey, calliope. how's it going?

-exhausting. i just spent the last hour being a chair. fucking, sadie sat on my back for an hour while

i was on all fours and i'm supposed to write a three-page essay on my choices for the scene.

-were you stable and supportive?

-no. i was bitchy and uncomfortable.

more people were filing in.

jesus, we were all just kids.

i was twenty-one and i thought i acted thirty. but we were all prenatal little self-important objects that deserved to be

moved constantly by ideas and sensations.
it was childish and yet very necessary.

and if we ever get a chance to live in madness and float in
a soup of odd flavors, we should always do so. if only for
a while.

episode 2

a

twisted

christmas

vibe

my apartment looked like this:

third-floor open walk-up, right by the stairs, and completely dark by the time i got there.

i had a long card table lined with totem spirits i made from
old bottle caps and cigarette packs.
beside it were two huge, bulky, house speakers bookend-
ing a tiny stereo.

to my right was a futon mattress on the floor in front of a
bookshelf that housed all my stolen books.

slightly further to the left was the bathroom where i shit
my pants once while throwing up in the toilet.
to the right was a closet with no clothes in it.

i was working really hard on being a drunk back then. my
weapon of choice was mickey's big mouths.

it was disgusting but god, you could get a six-pack for a
few bucks.

empty green bottles and red marlboro packs gave the
whole place a twisted christmas vibe.

after i passed out i woke up to the sound of a pounding
door. my door. when i opened it, it was nancy.

she was a middle-aged lady i worked with at walmart a few
months back.

she would bring me pills and booze cause i think she wanted
to fuck me but i never would.
but we'd sit and get high and drink on my futon mattress for
an hour or so.

then i'd make up some reason to get the hell out of there and
i'd walk her to the door.

episode 3

i

was

kind

of

a

dipshit

so, technically i had a job at a pizza place.

i say technically because my boss had not scheduled me in
two weeks.

it was becoming pretty clear that he just passive-aggressively
fired me.

i mean, i get it. i was kind of a dipshit.

but he never said anything and when i asked why i wasn't on
the schedule all he said was:
-we'll try and fit ya in.

i only asked about it that one time.

episode 4

and

fry

street,

of

course

it's a little northwest of dallas. at the crest of texas. that's
where most of these stories happened.
the groovy little town of denton.

and fry street, of course. where all the weird would flock and
nest for hours. drinking the coffee of youth.

until the dusk came. and then the whispers would get tangled
up in the night.
growing into anthems of booze and loud shadows. and we
would get all burned up from the heat.

leaving footprints on the ashes of the streets and our bodies.

like a phoenix caught fire and there were coyotes on the
moon.

episode 5

the

character

of

melted

cheese

and summers there were mean without humor and felt like heavy wet hands were always close to my face.

there was an actual pain to the heat which started shortly after dawn, got up to triple digits by noon, and held in the nineties at night.

when i moved there they were having record heat waves. and the weight of it all hanging on everybody just crippled ambition in the american spirit.

you couldn't move without misery.

the heat even had a smell. like warm muffins made of styrofoam being baked in shit.

that summer, before i got to denton i was in the belly of a 737 stuffing a 75lb. bag above my head on my knees suffocating by a blanket of hot breath.
i could have been just as easily back in ohio accepting my fate much sooner by getting some endless factory jobs full of gears and plastics.
but i thought being in the belly of a giant shiny oven was what i needed to build and shape my character at the time.

all i got was the character of melted cheese.
i acted like melted cheese.
shiny, shitty diner cheese that has been under a heat lamp too long.

this was not a beach boy's summer with surfboards in
bikinis.
this is texas airport summer, chucking heavy fucking bags
all over the world.

this was a summer that starts conversations
in lines about how different this summer was from other,
less noteworthy summers.

it was that hot. the honest factual temperature at this point
is irrelevant.
it can be any number that would make eyebrows rise in
the question of whether ears hear right.

whatever that degree is to you is how hot it was.
anyway, i was in what catholics call hell loading these
fucking bags...

episode *6*

he

was

a

hieroglyph

from

egypt

but back in denton, we rebuilt the town after the fire. like always.

and i was in the coffee shop again. it was home for most of the nonsense that got started back then.

it was right on fry street and that was where all the misfits were.
they had vintage arcade games and an old jukebox that seemed to play every song ever recorded all at once.

shit was carved and drawn into every square inch of space on the tabletops of booths.

so many different names wuz here.

also, there were dirty limericks about dolores. and poems on loneliness. the couples frozen in wood with arrows and hearts.

and the stick man was there, of course.
with his jagged, old body made of a thousand scratches.

drawn down over the years, by many hands. telling our stories in spiderwebs of scribbled motion.

he was a hangman in some. a cowboy. on skateboards. in hot rods. leaping from helicopters. fucking stick women. and other stick men, sometimes.

he was sitting on a crescent moon. and on the bottom of the
sea. with a single line going from his head to the surface.

he was stuck all over the tabletops of the coffee shop.

thought bubbles beside his blank faces.
word balloons cut out with pocket knives.

he was a hieroglyph from egypt.
acting out our little plays like shakespeare.

episode 7

like

sour

patch

kids

there was this one odd character that worked at the coffee shop.

his name was joe. i always called him coffee, joe? like a question. I said his name like i was offering him coffee.

he hated that i said his name like a question.

so, anyway, coffee, joe? believed he was abducted by aliens and that they shoved a bunch of gadgets in his ass to control the weather. he'd never shut up about it.

he was from cleveland, ohio and i only found that interesting because i was also from ohio.

we were both very far from anything near ohio.
so, i would attempt to bond with him over this shallow coincidence.

i would say things like,
-fucking ohio, am i right?

and he'd kinda spitefully shrug like he was dead inside and couldn't enjoy anything.

he was alright, though. we took some acid one night. and he played the band morphine till our brains became puckered little joy sockets. like sour patch kids... if that makes sense?

i heard later on that he moved to california and lived in his car for a while. far as i know he's still alive.

episode 8

my

o'keeffe

is

running

i guess, there was this girl i wanted to impress once.

we were on the third floor outside my door on the balcony just looking out at the night together.

tom waits was howling from my apartment about not wanting to grow up but we were still young then, so it didn't matter.

i get it in my head to put on my grey raincoat that i bought at a thrift store for three bucks. and a beat up old stetson that had perfect timing.

and i start calling myself the grey ghost and i'd hold the tail of the coat just under my eyes and laugh maniacally.

we both chuckled a bit and moved a little closer but not in a way you'd notice.
it's like eye contact till you're a foot apart and you don't know how you got there.

that kind of closer.

i got all nervous and i told her i bet i can climb down the side of the building.

we were both heavily intoxicated. and we both thought that was something we read in comic books.

so, then i went tripping down a wall of feet. laughing, with my grey raincoat swooshing and smacking the bricks.

i should have died, of course, but i didn't. and we laughed a lot more when i got down.
then we went back upstairs…

that girl. caroline. she was great. when she was on her period she would always say,
-my o'keeffe is running.

which is a brilliant line after she explained to me who georgia o'keeffe was and showed me her vagina fruit paintings.

we would spend days talking about everything.

just two floating spines with marble white eyes watching lips say pretty young words. laughing honey words. and her lips were worth watching.

she turned me on to many cool things. and we got together for a while.

but i was still too torn up from the last one to give her the attention she deserved.

i felt bad, of course, but it just wasn't right.

anyway, before any of that shitty stuff happened we were to-

gether all the time. so, she'll pop up here and there whenever it strikes me.

episode 9

the

night

i

shit

my

pants

the night i shit my pants while vomiting in the toilet was
bad before that.

it was already bad. that fact just capped the night.

it started at the pizza place i didn't work at but still got
free beer from.
the sympathetic employees sided with me on how our
boss/not boss handled matters.
in that, he hadn't handled shit.

so, i'd get free beer. and even at that tender age, i knew
this could be a problem later. but who turns down free
beer?

so, i drank. and i drank.

and i ended up at some crowded bar with people spilling
in the streets.

i was going to play pool and declared loudly to the person
next to me that,
-i'll make a five rail bank with the eight in the corner.

and i swished the tail of my raincoat back really dramatic
like i was a romanian count.

and this wonky voice next to me is mumbling about getting some pussy and i just want to shoot some pool.

but there was a problem.

i was very drunk and felt a sudden wave of claustrophobia
from the crowd and decided to get some coffee next door.

but as soon as i got outside i threw up. i felt the awful relief
exit me and seemed like a new man for a minute.

so, i walk inside the coffee shop and see a table of folks i
recognized and i order a cup and sit down with them.

there was a stick man with a flamethrower setting fire to the
name denise drawn on the table.

we start talking and then i slowly stop talking and then all
their voices seem to be swimming back and forth and i can't
understand what they're saying and my eyes are tennis balls
bouncing to any mouth that speaks.

and then the feeling in my guts came blustering so i shot up
and into the bathroom.

i wretched like i was giving birth to demons.

i got up. cleaned up.
and walked by the table, waving unsteadily,
-i'm out.

i hit the parking lot and immediately puke again. i stagger

a few yards and puke some more. all the while, grunting big, loud, gutty, grunts.

and there were people still walking around seeing all this. i finally get to my apartment and i puke on the landing.

now, i have to walk upstairs. three stories of stairs.

i crawl like a beggar to the second floor. i stand up and puke. i keep walking in sheer defiance at this point.
- fuck it, i yelled to a night that wasn't listening. i'm going to make it.

i get to the third floor and puke over the railing. but my room is right by the stairs. i'm home free.

i open the door and leap headfirst into the toilet.

and with one final blasted power chord of naked electricity. ripping through a triple stack of marshal amps. on a '58 cherry red fender. that was played by god himself. with his long white beard wagging in a staticky dance over the strings. an epic in glowing robes.

then a thunder came and leveled the mountains and it rang through my body like clanging bells.
and after fighting countless proud battles, over many long years, my poor defeated bowels emptied into my pants.

episode 10

a

dumb

easy

way

of

speaking

the first time i knew that i wanted to write, i was talking
to a friend, walking around town one night when i was
fifteen.

the three words that started this whole mess were:
-shaq that rim.

there was a children's basketball hoop maybe six ft. tall in
the yard of some house we were walking by.
and so, i used shaq as a verb to convey to my friend what i
wanted him to do to that rim.

a dumb easy way of speaking.

and, without saying anything, he runs over and annihilates
this kid's toy. leaving the hoop on the ground shattered.

i was shocked at how fast all that happened. i said something that he instantly understood. thought was a great
idea. and immediately executed without hesitation.

and now, some child is going to go outside the next morning to find their basketball hoop broken in pieces on the
ground.

the parents, who most likely bought the damn thing, probably had to listen to them crying.

these are things that can happen when you write for the

wrong audience.

i learned that night, on a gut level, the power of words.
we ran away really fast laughing and he was saying how cool
he thought it was. me telling him to shaq that rim.

how he'd never heard it said like that before and how he
thought that shit was really clever and i was getting kind of
proud of myself just arranging three little words together.

after that night, i started thinking about words more.
where they can go and what they can mean depending on the
place you put them.
so, then i started reading people who made a living moving
words around and shaqqing other people's rims with their
ideas.

and i thought that would be as good a thing to keep up as
anything else.

but we're never just dreamers, are we?

just think of all the toys we'd break.

episode 11

as

if

the

issue

had

been

settled

the norwegian was what we all called our dispatcher at american airlines. his first name was bill.

we never tried to pronounce his last name. we just always called him, the norwegian. like he was a fucking bond villain. it was his job to assign crews to a truck and a jet to clean. he was a sadist.

the shittiest truck we had was #26. it would always break down on the tarmac and we would have to call maintenance. then we would have to load up all the cleaning supplies we could and trudge to the jet on foot.

wherever it happened to be.

in the dead of summer, the tarmac could get up to 130 degrees.

it was august.
and the truck never seemed to break down anywhere close to the jet you were assigned.

everyone knew it was the worst and whoever got it would exhale very loudly when they got up to get their gear. and the norwegian would pick the people he hated most for #26.

he pulled my name for overtime and said i had that hunk of shit. i said i couldn't stay. i told him i had a doctor's appointment.

which was a lie.
he said he didn't care. which was the truth.

he said he pulled my name and i had to work.

 i said again that i couldn't and then apologized as if the
issue had been settled.

it was not.

he said that i was going to need to get my steward in-
volved. american was a union but had non-union supervi-
sors. so, any beef you had with a supervisor you had to go
whine to your steward.
i walk down the hall and tell the steward what i had just
told the norwegian. he asked me about the nature of the
doctor's appointment.

so, i had to make up something quick. i tell him that i have
to get tested for an std. that my penis had gloppy green
paste seeping out of it and i was worried.

he is writing all this down as i tell him.

so, somewhere a file exists on my seeping green dick at
american.

the steward gets his ducks in a row.

now, all three of us have to sit in an office while he defends my case. he has to tell the norwegian that i have to get my dick looked at without ever using those words.

he said things like: unavoidable and dire. and i nodded in very somber ways to express how truly regretful i felt but how very necessary this visit was... whatever it was.

so, finally, the norwegian caved and said i could leave. that was pretty much my last day, anyway. 9/11 happened and we all got canned. as i got on the highway and turned up the radio, van morrison was half a mile from the county fair and i noticed that the sun looked nicer in air conditioning.

episode 12

his

name

tag

said,

beak

one flight i was cleaning with this italian guy, a nigerian, and two black kids my age.

the italian guy acted like a real good fella.
he was from new york.
he was big and booming and funny.

which annoyed everybody else but i ate that shit up. at least, he was doing something. it made the cleaning go faster. we were horsing around and he started calling me a honky and white trash because i was from ohio and he was from new york and that's what people from ohio were to people from new york. cousin fuckers with belt buckles.

there are still plenty of those in ohio.

so, i start thinking of every derogatory italian thing i could to hit him with. and the two black kids start chuckling and shit. and italy and i are laughing but the nigerian never looks up from cleaning and never even smiles. he just keeps working away.

after a while, we're all wondering why he's not laughing.

i mean, we were all saying some pretty hilarious shit at this point.

but he never looks up. so, i asked him,
    -jesus, beak…

his name tag said, beak.

i think it was because he was obsessed with donald duck.
he had a donald duck pocket watch that he would wind
constantly. in a therapeutic type way. you could tell it
helped him.

my name tag said, pink. because of the floyd beanie i wore
all the time.

i say;
-jesus, beak. why aren't you rolling? this shit is gold.

and he looked up with wet eyes and said that his wife
happened to be from ohio. and that he met her walking out
of a movie theater in dayton twelve years ago, when he
first moved to america.

he said it was the little mermaid. beak really loved disney,
i guess. especially donald duck. he said they collected all
the toys and shit. they both did. he was a sweet, weird guy.
and she loved him.

but he said that she passed away six months ago from
cancer and mentioning ohio must have opened a spicket
in him and then he apologized to us as if he'd done something wrong.

and then we all loudly apologized back saying,

-oh, shit. we didn't know. and,
 -fuck, man. i'm sorry.

then it got really quiet in the cabin because everything had
already been said. and it was awkward and tense and weird.
and we all became characters in his story.

the four of us, holding this silence like a halo above beak's
head. hoping that holding it would help the memories simmer
and not hurt as much.

he seemed to calm down and we started lightly talking and
snickering but not like before.
just simple easy talk that bounces out without much effort. he
even joined in a little this time. we made sure to let him tell
us whatever he had to say.

episode 13

this
gang
of
faces

the very first time i tripped was still the most important. because my mind's hymen exploded.

i know, it's lewd.

but it spilled all over in a technicolor splash. the sky shut-
tered and flocked like birds of memories with their feathers
the colors of different days i've been alive.
they nestled in golden fleecy trees, dripping in the wet virgin
sun. feeling it pop inside a new universe. and then out in a
warm flowing womb of fingers.

 it took forever to hit, but when it did:
bam!!!

my buddy and i had bought an ounce earlier that day and a
bag of weed to kill time till the rabbit came out.

an hour into it, i was high but still not tripping. so, i asked my
friend, who had done it before, when this shit was going to
kick in.
 and, like clockwork, the tv we were watching starts flashing
this gang of faces going back and forth like a duck hunt on
the screen.

and the faces had their hands cupping their cheeks as they
howled:
yap, yap, yap, yap, yap.
louder than anything else in the room.

and i looked across at my buddy on the couch, whose smile started curling up like the witches' legs when doro-thy took her slippers.

just coiling snakes of skin grinning back at me.

then all of the screaming stopped.

and i ask him if he sees the faces and he says that he is seeing something else. and that we won't see the same things but that we are still on the same trip.

and how that's ok.

and that the buzzing faces are actually spores of fungus attacking your brain.

and that this is how your brain fights back.
and that this tug of war is the trip.
and once you come back from the trip, the war will have always been worth it.

because the violence done to your brain is no different than saltwater shaping a coastline.

or the magma glass that stiffens and reflects the topaz of a sunset.

and i just nodded like my grandmother used to with her preacher. and saw that some lies only hurt if you let them.

episode 14

so

often

wrong

about

so

many

things

when i was a kid i always wanted to be a private eye.

i never wanted to be a cop.

they seemed uncomfortable with all that stuff on.
the best private eyes didn't even need a gun until maybe the
end of the episode.

they would spend the whole show interviewing people, track-
ing down leads, most of the time with a hangover, and would
still always figure it out long before the cops ever did.

 because they didn't have to play by the rules. i liked that a
lot as a kid.

that there were guys out there that didn't mind breaking the
law for the greater good.
they saw the big picture and if they waited on a warrant that
poor girl would die in the cellar.

so, they transcended the laws of man because men are so
often wrong about so many things.

there are some good rules too. don't get me wrong.

most of history has been marked by big dick swings. and
we've all met people that would fit right in with attila the
hun.

and had they been born in worse places, they would have gladly been a warlord that threw newborns in a river.

but instead, they got jobs in factories or the service industry or some other fucking thing besides what they really want to do.

and believe me, they are cold-blooded killers just acting normal. sometimes they even dress like cops.

episode 15

small
polished
stones

i liked playing go at the coffee shop with a guy i called
john the fascist.

i called him that because he was always reading nietzsche
and ayn rand. and i couldn't stand either one of them.

he was always quoting them to show girls how much of an
intellectual he was. i mean, i quoted writers i liked too but
their books were better.

it just seemed like those two assholes encouraged the
worst parts of people. like they would get in the dark
nooks and crannies of a fella's head and lay webby spores
that have been bad in folks since the beginning.

that shit doesn't need to be encouraged if we're going to
make it as a species, if you ask me.

anyway, we'd play go. i'd like to think i was in a battle
against the icy grip of stalin and i was toppling a global
maniac.

except that he was really good and i was really bad. i don't
think i ever won.
the stick man on the table had his arms crossed like he was
judging me. i could've sworn he was shaking his head.

i came from chess and didn't get the slow spread of posi-
tioning and long-term strategy that go needs.

my small polished stones would link in a thin chain and his stones would envelop my stones every time.

he really hated that i called him a fascist.

i would introduce him to people as john the fascist and he would shoot this really shitty look at me.

and i'd just laugh and say,
-i'm fucking with you. lighten up.

he pulled me outside the coffee shop one night after doing this and said:

-man, you gotta stop calling me a fucking fascist. the girls don't like that shit.

he was the guy with me at the bar the night i shit myself who wanted pussy when i just wanted to play pool.

i say:
-c'mon man. all you ever talk about is pussy and politics and quote the fountainhead, scamming chicks into thinking you're deep.

that really pissed him off and he suddenly got all puffy and antsy. i try to calm him down but he's remembering every time i ever called him john the fascist and he just gets more pissed.

and i'm thinking,
fuck, this fascist is about to hit me. i talk a lot of shit but i
don't fight. but he finally calms down a little and we walk
back inside.
we go back to the table i'd just introduced him to and said,
-whatever you do, don't call him a fascist. he's gonna rule
the world someday.

episode 16

burnt

orange

caterpillars

perth was a hippie kid with dreads that always had the best
weed.

he was named after that city in australia. he turned me
onto some great indie bands like king missile and the asy-
lum street spankers.

he worked in the cafeteria at school but his folks paid for
everything. so, he spent all his money on top-shelf shit.
one day i was at his place and he said he's going to make a
run and had me hang tight there. after a little while, i hear
him pull in.

i go to the front door, open it, and get pummeled by the
funkiest odor i have ever encountered.

this i could smell through a double wrapped bag in a paper
sack in his pocket.

i say:
-jesus, what the fuck is that? is it safe to smoke? do i have
to sign something first?
-yeah, man. you're about to sign your life away.
and he gives me this look; not sinister… i think the right
word is puckish.

like a trickster's grin. and he takes this tiny nug and lays it
soft as a pillow in his pipe.

adds fire, inhales, and instantly blasts a giant cloud into my
face.

hacking out plumes of dancing smoke mixed with spit. his
watered-red eyes cascaded beautiful tears of euphoric joy.

now, it's my turn and he hands me the pipe.
i'm a little intimidated. i smoked dirt weed and was glad to
have that.

this was some mutant strand with burnt orange caterpillars
wrapping their furry legs around every bud.

but i took a long pull and held the fucker in tight with everything i got. and just like a train barreling out the side of a
mountain, i blew a fat stack straight up.

it swirled around the room and in my brain. i sank inside my
raincoat like a cocoon and for a while, i was happy.

episode 17

we

learn

how

to

fall

perth and i ended up at some old victorian house one night.

we were sitting on a very large wraparound front porch and it was pitch black outside. he was wearing my raincoat because earlier he used it to swipe beer from the gas station.

it was probably two in the morning. and we were shooting the shit with a couple of stragglers that happened to be there. and perth had to take a leak. so, he gets up to piss by the side of the house.

he walks off the front porch, and suddenly vanishes like he was swallowed up whole, with the flaps of my raincoat swooshing out and him disappearing in the quick, black night.

followed by:
-fuck! with an oof and the sounds of crumpled heavy thuds...
we found out later that the owner had been working on the stairs until his wife left him and then he went to shit. so, there were no stairs.

we had entered through the back door. and of course, we had been drinking and it was very dark. and there were no porch lights. so, perth didn't see the drop and hadn't prepared for a fall. and it was a tall porch.

he was expecting the stairs to exist at that moment. which seemed reasonable to me.

and as i watched him disappear that night, under a charcoal moon; i was thinking that bodies were actually helpless without wings…

i just remember the way his flailing body fell and then vanished. that was really shocking to me. it was sudden and completely against his will.
his arms were grabbing for anything, firing the same old synapses that always tries to keep everything alive. all at once. everyday...

and then fails. horribly and constantly.

anyway, i watched perth try to stop this thing from happening and then lose, really hard. but the body survives, so we learn how to fall.

i respect that fight. the one fight that we all feel in our guts.
 and then, the bastard was laughing as he got up.

episode 18

between

shots,

i'd

look

up

when i was ten my cousin tried to beat me to death with a baseball bat.

i've had trust issues ever since.

he was my younger cousin but i was a scrawny, little kid and he was a fat pile of shit.

everyone in the family knew he was a violent sociopath.
his dad was also a violent sociopath.
without knowing the words, i knew.

i could never be alone around him for long because he would inevitably get this crazy, menacing grin on his face and try something.

and that time, we were in my aunt's backyard playing and he snuck up behind me and just started wailing away on my head and body.

i couldn't fight back because i was already on the ground. between shots, i'd look up and he had this far away stare like he was swinging through me and hitting something he really wanted to kill.

i start fucking screaming as loud as i could until the family heard and our uncle ran over and pulled him off of me.
otherwise, i'm pretty sure he wouldn't have stopped, even after i was dead.

i was kind of bloody and confused at the hate a child
shouldn't understand.

 i just knew it was scary to see his eyes like that. beating me
to get at some devil in his head.
i was wondering why he didn't like me. why he would want
to hurt me.

 and you only figure this shit out when you get older and start
to get why most of it has nothing to do with you. and that
fucked up part of a child's brain was put there by a fucked up
parent in most cases.
and killing me was a moment he got to. because it was easier
than killing his old man.

so, i still see him, every now and then at family reunions. and
we bullshit and laugh about what a psycho he used to be. and
it's cool.
because our childhoods are always there to remind us how
small we are.

episode **19**

that

was

supposed

to

be

hell

i was at the coffee shop one day writing a story about this guy i named barnabas fathum.

the stick man in the corner of the table was walking off a cliff down into a pit of ten thousand scribbles that was supposed to be hell.

i made barnabas own this magical pub that lonely people would wander into and then disappear forever.

this pub would squeeze into a street somewhere just long enough to grab a few patrons and poof.
it would vanish.

fathum would take all these sad broken people to the land of the faeries. and there, they would be fed to the queen of the faeries.

because centuries ago, fathum lost a wager to the queen which cost him his freedom. and now, he delivers these poor lost souls to their doom.

i wanted to make barnabas rebel against her. because he was not a bad man. This enchanted place was for the people that had nowhere else to go. It was never meant for this.

i wanted him to finally stop this horrible thing he'd been made to do by the queen and i guess, me.

maybe, one of them at the pub could be a woman, i
thought. and it would stir in him something he believed
was long dead and all that shit.
but it didn't feel genuine. because it had felt done to death,
by writers better than me.

so, barnabas kept on taking these sad broken people to the
queen and she would eat them. bones and all.
and more centuries have passed and he keeps taking these
poor lost souls to the banks of avalon. and they are still
being devoured by the queen of the faeries.

all because i can't decide why not...

episode 20

little

planets

after i got evicted, i lived with caroline for a while.
i was going back to ohio.

i started depending on people too much. and you never
want to be the last one to notice that.

we were all just little planets in a parking lot of stars. shar-
ing orbits and theories and bad habits.

episode 21

and

the

chestnuts

and

the

open

fires

but before i was evicted i was still living in my apartment that christmas.

three other guys and i were in the midst of a five-day bender leading up to the birth of santa claus or something.

i woke up christmas morning with my raincoat wrapped around me and empty bottles and bodies laying all over the floor.

i tap coffee, joe? on the back of his head with my foot and he looks up with these bee-swarmed eyes and groggy voices,

-what the fuck!!! with such a hissing whisper, that i let him sleep.

i step over another guy by the front door. and i walk outside into the full light of day and see there's been a splotchy dusting of snow. with car-packed patches of slag- ging shit brown ice all over the place.

so, i was standing at the balcony of my third floor apart- ment. christmas morning.

a million miles from anything like home. barely alive from all this booze, breathing out cold smoke from my first morning cigarette and slipping down all the branches of life...

and from inside, i can hear nat king cole on the radio. and the chestnuts. and the open fires.

and i thought, this was as good a day as any for a miracle.

episode 22

that
first
fuzzy
crackle

zelda was a card-carrying member of the communist party.

i know this because she showed me the card. she liked to show everyone the card. she was pretty proud of it.

she'd never been to a meeting or anything. she just sent away for the card and it came in the mail. maybe she paid dues like a union.
i don't know.
zelda had a friend with her from high school at the coffee shop.

they'd both gone to the same high school and now were in college together.
she kept calling him pigshit but his name was nathan.

i know this because he would correct her every time he was introduced that way.

they never explained why she called him pigshit. and I didn't ask.
but you don't get a name like that lapping through snow. and here was zelda reminding strangers about it.

i am pretty sure that nathan felt a real fear that he would never be anything other than that pigshit from high school.

the stick man on the table played a violin with musical notes floating out of it.

we all went back to his place and listened to hip-hop re-
cords and snorted some coke that pigshit had.

he was a wiry guy before the coke. he had these giant ex-
cited eyes that would bulge out with rippled temple veins
pulsing. he was an intense dude.

he starts freestyle rapping in front of us.

it wasn't bad if you like rap. zelda didn't look impressed.
she was flipping through a magazine really fast. i felt like
my brain was being sandblasted.

-what do you think, man? i just got the speakers.
-yeah, good shit, man, i said.
it was a nice system.
-what do you listen to?
-i like dylan.
-dylan? i fucking love dylan!

and pigshit runs over to his crate of vinyl and pulls out
blood on the tracks.

he said he got it at a yard sale for fifty cents. it wasn't my
favorite of his back then. pigshits, either.

i was still listening to the electric sixties rimbaud guy all
the time. spiraling new nebulas of words in blacked out
shades and screaming hair.

i knew for a fact that bob was the first punk that ever mattered and before him everything was oobiedoobie bullshit
and even the beatles were a boy band. but i couldn't prove
that without getting booed every time.

but i also thought that bob was already an old man with nothing left to say by the time he'd made these tracks.

i was just a shit kid who hated everything and couldn't know
what life can do to songs when you can't ignore them anymore.

i would ignore songs all the time back then.

pigshit put it on and that first fuzzy crackle led into tangled
up in blue.

we listened to bob talk about this girl.

and how it didn't last but should have. and how whenever he
would come to a new town he'd always have to leave again
because he just didn't feel at home anywhere and there was
never a good reason to stay anyway.

and all the time there was this girl that he was trying to get
back to.

the whole damn thing was about her.

every place he'd been and all the freaks he'd met that
burned up on the road, were just accidents on his way
back to her.

but he never got there again.
and i got to hear him live through that.

learning how to heal the parts that die and turning that hurt
into some bridges of verse.

 it helps me sometimes when i need it to.

it was a song i couldn't ignore.

episode 23

boxer

on

a

leash

i saw my ex one day walking around town.

she lived across campus so we rarely saw each other
which was fine by me. she cheated on me with some barista at the starbucks we all worked at then.

i met her when i worked there. she was outside wearing
these large breakfast at tiffany's type sunglasses and she
was pulling a boxer on a leash.

she comes in and orders. she told me later that she thought
i was a dick to her the first time we met but i was actually
just really nervous because she was so beautiful.

anyway, we start hanging out and she eventually gets a job
with me and suddenly we're together all the time. we're
just friends at first. talking and going places and learning
about each other.

she wasn't from there, either. she was from california.
which was a lot nicer and more cultured and all around
just leagues better than anything here, according to her.
if we didn't know what the word, 'elitist' meant, we would
have just called her a bitch.

but she was beautiful. and well-read. she had quite a library that i devoured. i eventually got the nerve to ask her
out and we hooked up that night, right in the driveway of
my aunt's house. which i was living at then.

she got real worked up doing it out in public. and i didn't care at all.

i got a ticket one time because she was giving me head when i was passing a cop and i kinda gave him this knowing little wink as we passed him and we were both completely naked.

he whips it around and throws on the lights. we scrambled to get our clothes on as he approached. i pulled up my pants and gave her my raincoat cause she couldn't find her shirt.

he got me for a seatbelt violation and let us go.

one time we fucked in the chaplain's office at the airport when i used to work for american airlines while someone was trying to come in but i had her pressed real good against that door until they went away.

we finished. cleaned up.

and i walked out holding her head to my chest as if she'd been crying.

there were bathrooms at starbucks. changing rooms in thrift stores.
against a car that wasn't ours.

it didn't matter where it was and that was pretty liberating.
but we fought all the time when we weren't fucking.

to her, i was just a backward midwestern loser who knew nothing.
anything would set her off on some fucking tangent then we'd start arguing and get all worked up and we'd fuck.

that seemed like such a reasonable pattern that we repeated it for two years.
till we split up.

but anyway, i saw her walking around town that day.

she had dyed her hair blonde. it had been black. leaving me made her brighter. i get it.

i try to avoid her seeing me so i duck into the coffee shop.
i sit down at a table with a stick man giving me the finger.
and not five minutes later she walks in and looks right at me.

she walks up kind of snotty with a twisted snap to her steps. she says,
-what are you doing here? i thought you were moving back to ohio.
-no. i got rent for a couple more months and i like it here. the people are interesting. besides, i got nowhere else to be.

just then, calliope walks up and gets all flirty with me in front of my ex and it's hilarious. i had told calliope about my ex before. so, she did me a solid and laid it on real thick.

and my ex just kinda says goodbye in one of those ways that means forever. because it was.

episode 24

like

a

mouse

pissin'

on

cotton

it was kind of a fluke that i ended up in college in the first place.

it was my ex that pushed me to get in. i had no business being there, though. i barely graduated high school.

 my last two years were in an automotive lab at a vocational school. learning to loosen and tighten bolts. all i did was get really high before class and stand around wrenches and hammers.

complete waste of my parent's money. i just never learned too much in school. it seemed very congested and confusing. and i would always get distracted by the least damn thing.

now, this girl. the ex.

she was on a trajectory in life and wouldn't waste her body on an uneducated oaf like me unless i agreed to apply to college with her.

anyway, i applied. they rejected me.
i was not shocked but had to act sad. so, i shrugged my shoulders to my ex like,
-whatterrryaagunnaadooo?

this did not assuage her fear that i was an idiot, at all. in fact, my la de da approach to everything about school, really rubbed her the wrong way.

but this wasn't part of the plan. i moved to texas in the first place because my aunt and uncle got me a job at american airlines.

and i was staying with them till i got on my feet. but i met this girl and fucked that all up. the real problem was my grades from high school. they were god awful and no damn university would take that.

so, the ex tells me that i have to write a letter when i reapply because my grades were so bad.
so, i wrote about shooting pool like it was a metaphor for life.
how the balls are objects in your way to the goal. and how anyone can make a couple shots but to get from the one to the nine, consistently, you had to plan several shots ahead.

the focus isn't on the object but what the object is in the way of.
don't shoot the three straight in or you'll never get shape on the four.

my uncle always said to kiss it in. keep it simple, stupid. that's good advice.
there is a specific sequence in every game that will win. it might only take one hard shot to drop the rest. and that's what i'm looking for: the kiss that puts it in. the most effective way to sink the nine and collect all the money.

that's life, baby.

or at least, that's the shit i shoveled for the acceptance com-
mittee…

my uncle was the one who taught me to play pool. taught all
my cousins, too. this wasn't the uncle i lived with in texas. it
was my father's older brother. back in ohio.
he was kind of an eccentric guy. he got all fucked up in viet-
nam from too many high altitude jumps.

he was an airborne ranger. he also used to be in a biker gang
and had a spider tattooed on his hand which was the insignia
of the club.

he said he once shot a man as he was crossing a bridge with
a pistol. and after he shot the guy, he had to throw his body
over the bridge.

and then he would show me that same pistol.

 he had a lot of pistols.
he had a lot of guns. and knives.

he watched a lot of war movies starring john wayne and
glenn ford. he had two doberman pinschers he named chop-
per and zorba.

my mother had told me that he tried to commit suicide in

front of her once, with a kitchen knife.
i hadn't been born yet.

but my mother and older sister, who was a baby then,
were living with my uncle and his wife while my father
was in basic training for the army.

i guess, my uncle and his wife were fighting and he
grabbed a knife in front of the whole house and stabbed
and slashed at himself until they could wrestle the blade
from him.

when he was very young he almost drowned in a swimming pool. he just laid there at the bottom and they had to
pull his blue body out. and i guess, he hadn't been right
ever since.

he had a very active imagination.

but he was very good at shooting pool. when i would
make a pretty decent shot, he would scream loudly,
-like a mouse pissing on cotton!

he had a lot of great lines like that. and when he got really
drunk he would quote the bible... sort of. he'd say,
-when you know, you know that you know. when you
don't know, you don't even... know... you... don't...
know!!!

and he would always bellow that last part out real slow and
fucking loud to emphasize his point.

so, i sent this letter about playing pool to an actual university
and they accepted me.

i was shocked.

 i bullshitted the whole thing and they bought it.
now, i have to go to fucking school again. which, as i said,
was not part of the plan. i learned nothing in college except
where most of my classes were.

 i never went to class. i never read the assignments. i would
show up on test day and fail. every class was like that.
i was too distracted by the newness of everything.

and how exciting it was attending a university. and having a
girlfriend that i fucked constantly.
all that classroom stuff with a stiff professor just wasn't for
me.

this is all twenty years of rationalizing, of course.

but at that time in my life, i was living in brand new skins.
alive with nothing but stupid, brave innocence.
and all of that eventually gets beaten up and called wisdom
later, of course. if you're lucky or care enough to look back at
all.

and my uncle was right.

if you live your whole life never knowing, you aren't even aware of what you missed. but it's ok, most people don't know on purpose.

episode 25

all

of

their

pictures

would

vanish

now, i might as well tell you about my other uncle. my father's younger brother. he only had the two.

his name was rocky. he's dead now.

most of my relatives are. but when he was alive, jesus. he was insatiable. i was with him the whole day right up till he died.

i was sixteen. just got my license and he'd just gotten a dui. we were all driving up to my aunt's house for easter but he wanted to leave a day early to play golf with a cousin of mine up there. my aunt's son.

so, he asked if i'd drive him. and i looked up to my uncle as a hero and of course i said i would.

we got on the road and it was great. the whole memory of it is perfect. like something that deserves to be framed behind glass.
he told me about music and women and drinking and fighting in bars with assholes whose women he stole.

we laughed the whole ride.

and it was the best way to say goodbye to someone when you didn't know they were about to die.

when we got there he stuck me with my aunt and some

family that had arrived early too. then he went to play golf with my cousin.

later that night; maybe ten, my aunt gets the call and we all scramble to the hospital. and my aunt keeps mumbling, no heartbeat, no brainwaves, as she's driving.

but she keeps praying to jesus. and saying, please god don't take him.

we drove by the red neon glow of the emergency sign and its reflection hit my aunt's wet face, making her cheeks look all bloody from the tears.
we run in and see him.

and it's a carcass. he's gone.
whatever he was, it wasn't that.

the body had some purple stains on it's chest and the face had a black eye and a broken nose. but other than that, it looked like him. just the meat and bones of what he used to be. same as clay can look like skin, if you make it.

my cousin was there.

he said that his girlfriend and him went into a grocery store and left rocky in the car. and that, at some point rocky got behind the wheel and drove the car into a brick wall in the parking lot. going about thirty miles an hour, we found out later. the steering wheel caved his chest in and crushed his heart on impact.

it came out later, that he had coke in his system and a shit ton of booze. cops ruled it a suicide. maybe, it was. accidental suicide out of his brain on chemicals. who knows?

maybe he was depressed. i don't know. he seemed pretty damn happy the whole trip up.

maybe, he was hotdogging. ripping ass through the parking lot. which he'd been known to do. maybe, he fucked up and lost control.

i can't say. i just think about my uncle, now and then. and the dumb sudden ways people can die, all at once. and forever.

the family never really hung out like we used to after that. we would all look around for him at get togethers and he wouldn't be there. everybody would look.

but then, he wouldn't be there. so, no one said anything. we were all too busy looking for a ghost.

that night, after we knew he had died, my aunt thought it would be too insensitive to call everyone on the phone with the news. so, another uncle and i made a midnight trek to each of our relatives' houses across half of the state.

waking them up one by one, to tell them that rocky was dead.
whoever he was to them; uncle, son, brother, father. i think it
was eight or nine houses by the time i got back home. it was
almost dawn.
and i still had to tell my father that his baby brother had just
died suddenly.

it was easter sunday and i was exhausted.
i hadn't slept.

i pulled into my folk's driveway and it was already full of
cars.

it was very selfish of me in that split second, seeing those
cars. because i was so relieved that my father already knew.
and i didn't have to tell him.

the people we told had gotten dressed and started leaving to
tell other people. like a pony express of bad news.

or a relay race, as someone hands you a stick with 'rocky is
dead' on it. and you run, because others need to know.

i walk in the house and see my father with his teary face,
surrounded by other teary faces and he breaks down and my
mom breaks down and i break down again after being broken
all night but too wired to stop.
we all squeezed each other, because we needed to feel living
things between us. we needed to warm up. because death is

so damn cold.

and then all the family finally ended up at my parent's house to make all the arrangements and cry some more together and hug each other some more times.

just maybe, make it so we didn't notice when one of us was gone.

they could just kind of disappear one day and all of their pictures would vanish and we would forget about them and that hurt feeling of letting go wouldn't happen anymore.

like windshield wipers scraping off bugs. so you can see better. because cars don't notice when a parking lot is empty.

my uncle's dead. i know that. i'm still dying. and so are you.

i'd like to save a life one day. any life. it might as well be yours.

i could leap in traffic like a madman, grabbing you just in time. then disappear in the crowd as you look around for me.

and you would tell your friends and family till the end about this strange angel that saved you.

with your pictures still hanging. safe in their frames.

episode 26

a

note

pinned

to

her

clothes

one time my ex told me that her friend ran over an old lady once and killed her. the old lady was committing suicide and had a note pinned to her clothes.

she chose some random car to jump in front of and it just happened to be my ex's friend. i thought that was a hell of a thing to lay on somebody you'd never even met.

the note said how she'd failed at everything she'd ever tried. and that she was barren for years and how she just wanted to give her love to something that needed her.

because nothing needed her.

and that she felt hollow like an empty house. just a body full of echoes. deep as a well. and that she couldn't go on being such a tragedy anymore.

so, she decided that anyone had to do it for her.
that anyone who did it would never forget. and that she was willing to shatter anyone's brain for the rest of their life.

and finally be someone to somebody. in a very fucked up way.

if it was truly random then anyone would have to do it. she couldn't do it herself.

and we were waiting for her to pick one of us without even

knowing it.
 no one could refuse because we didn't know which one of
us it would be.

neither did she.

anyone can speed down the road and fold an old woman's
body in half under their car until she stops breathing and
her heart stops beating.

anyone can do that.
that's the genius of it.

that's why this story isn't about my ex's friend.
it's about anyone.
which includes everyone.

just imagine if you were them. driving every day, everywhere, all the time. like most fucking people, i imagine.
and this bitch chose you. or me. anyone...

there isn't enough shit going on?
now, we have to see her jump in our lives.

with her eyes like fast cameras recording our faces and we
have to feel the bones snap and tumble under the weight
of the car? and hear that awful thumping underneath? now,
we have to live with that?

fuck every atom of that bitch for making strangers do what cowards can't.

and her selfishness has to include everything. and her good-bye is a lifetime of nightmares for someone.

it's medication and far off stares in elevators and awkward pauses with dinner guests because we see her face again, right there. screaming dead every time…

she left a smashed messy scab in the road. drug with ten yards of blood and skin like a slip n' slide behind her. she wanted to die leaving all her tire marks and twisted bones. she wanted to hurt the world back, for not needing her.

she screamed in all our faces, as she leapt in front of all our cars. dying in a way that really makes you hate sadness.

but we still don't need her.

she didn't mean anything to anyone except the poor bastard that flattened her.
you wouldn't even know about her if i hadn't told you and i only know from my ex.

episode 27

the

moon

looks

nicer

when

it's

full

dying quiet in a comfy bed with a few people around you isn't harmless, either. but it's easier to let go of. for the ones that are left.

none of this is really necessary. and it can end anytime we'd like. and the fact it's that easy, usually scares the bejesus out of most people.

then they go on vacation a few weeks a year and take a lot of pictures. snapping pictures like they're filling a balloon at the fair with a water pistol.

filling a clown's mouth with reasons to live. and the pictures they take are in frames in their homes.

so, i guess we just keep filling it up. because the moon looks nicer when it's full.

and i remember as a kid, tracing a spiral around that moon, on the dewey glass of my childhood windows.

i would start at the fuzzy glow that mirrored my face and then i would smear it away. squeaking my fingertip in slow circles, until nothing was left but the real moon outside.

and there it would be: an improbable sphere of side effects and gravity. hanging in the clouds on my window.

it was scarred and battered by eons of ancient fists from an

endless milky way. and beaten round like an old prize-
fighter. shining for no damn reason at all.

episode 28

it

was

blurry

but

it

was

happening

it was a breezy but warm afternoon that new year's eve.
the sun had taken care of most of the snow by then.

caroline and i were at the coffee shop just bullshitting.
we were sitting across from each other in a booth and the
back of her booth had a stick man on a trampoline bouncing from one arch to the other.

my neighbor, who lived with some roommates in a big
house behind my apartment, walked up and invited us to a
party he was throwing that night.

he was kind of an asshole but he had good taste in music
and a stocked bar. i had worked with him at starbucks, too.

he was always slick as an eel to my ex and a fucking prick
to me. so, there was friction but no outright animosity. far
as i know, she hadn't fucked him.

we get there at dusk and the place was already pregnant
with people. slobberbone's barrel chested was exploding
with that crunchy opening riff when we opened the door.

bodies were splashing in and out of each other. it was a
big house and it was full. the music was too loud to talk
without yelling. which i did to caroline.

-i need a drink! yelling over the speakers and other people
yelling.

so, we head to the kitchen and perth pops around the corner and kisses me on the mouth.

-what the hell, man? i chuckle, wiping my jaw.
-it's an orgy, motherfucker!!!

and everyone cheered when they heard that. i make a drink to catch up with the madness. i throw down a few to get started and we mix in with the other crazies.

i leaned in and kissed caroline because it felt like a moment to kiss someone and she let me.

i looked over and saw lorgo. he was a fire-breather in a traveling carnival.

and there was curvy frank, a satanic filmmaker. that's what he called himself. whatever that was.
he tried to explain it to me but the music was too loud and i wasn't really listening.

calliope was there, of course. she ran around giving everyone holy communion with tabs of acid as the flesh of christ.

coffee, joe? was over in the corner with a guy called father marsha. who was an emaciated, teenage jesus that sucked dick for money and would brag about it.

he wore a priest's collar around his neck everywhere he went.

i think he was a junky, too.

john the fascist ripped open his shirt and screamed. he had elaborate japanese dragons all over his chest. he may have been a yakuza.

there was also this guy, sundy. he was just learning guitar back then and had at least five girls on the couch with him while he strummed something no one could hear.

but it didn't matter, because nothing mattered.

except for the night and all that was happening and because everything seemed to be sped up.

like when you're driving and look to the side and see how fast you're really moving. because nothing in your windshield has happened yet but this is happening right now.

and the telephone poles are blurry whips when you pass them but when you look down the road they're a thousand arms stretching out wires with human voices inside of them.

and what you are seeing is just how fast you are moving.

that night, i saw how fast everything was moving. it was blurry but it was happening.

i looked around and said,
-i will remember this. until the sun eats the earth.

and fuck. i guess it all mattered and it always will have mattered.

because it's twenty years later and it's still happening all the time in places that are easy to touch and still feel like sandcastles…

later on, when it was dying down and we were taking off, it started raining. and i was wearing my good ole' raincoat.

so, i went out running in the rain, with my coat flapping like a cape and caroline ran with me.
we held hands still running and we laughed at all the flickering bodies splashing off the lampposts.

and then, when the rain fell hardest, we fizzled away like fireflies in the night. leaving our shadows burnt into the foggy street.

that's how all the best stories end.

www.ingramcontent.com/pod-product-compliance
Lightning Source LLC
Chambersburg PA
CBHW060650260626
47161CB00008B/3082